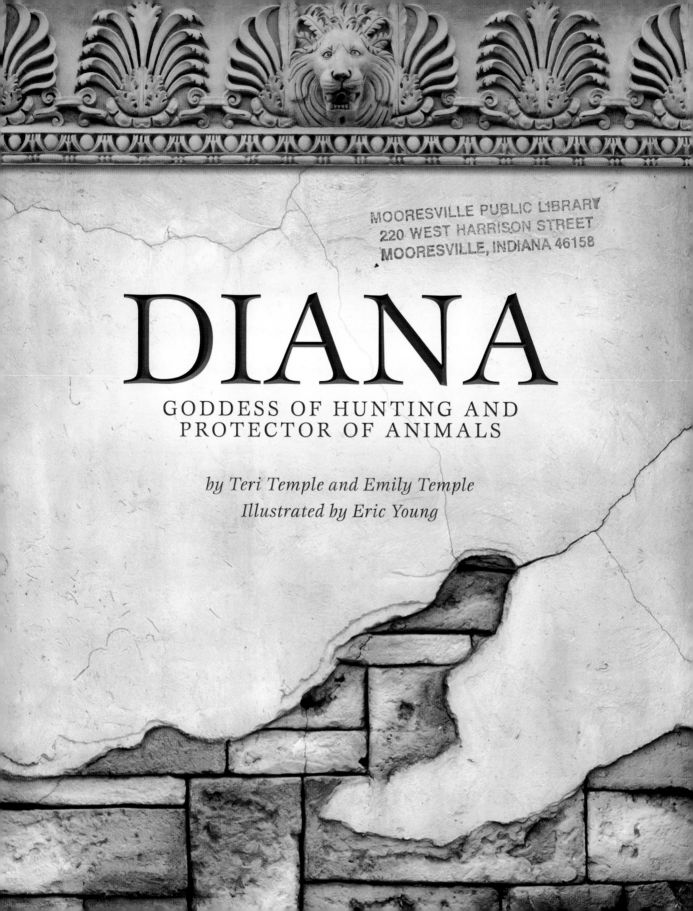

DIANA

GODDESS OF HUNTING AND PROTECTOR OF ANIMALS

by Teri Temple and Emily Temple

Illustrated by Eric Young

Published by The Child's World®
1980 Lookout Drive • Mankato, MN 56003-1705
800-599-READ • www.childsworld.com

ACKNOWLEDGMENTS
The Child's World®: Mary Berendes, Publishing Director
Red Line Editorial: Editorial direction
The Design Lab: Design and production
Design elements ©: Banana Republic Images/Shutterstock Images; Shutterstock
Images; Anton Balazh/Shutterstock Images
Photographs ©: Viacheslav Lopatin/Shutterstock Images, 5; Thinkstock, 12;
Kenneth Keifer/Shutterstock Images, 15; Helen Stratton, 17; Johann Bayer, 21;
Guillaume Rouille, 24; Shutterstock Images, 28

ISBN 9781631437168
LCCN 2014945439

Printed in the United States of America
Mankato, MN
November, 2014
PA02241

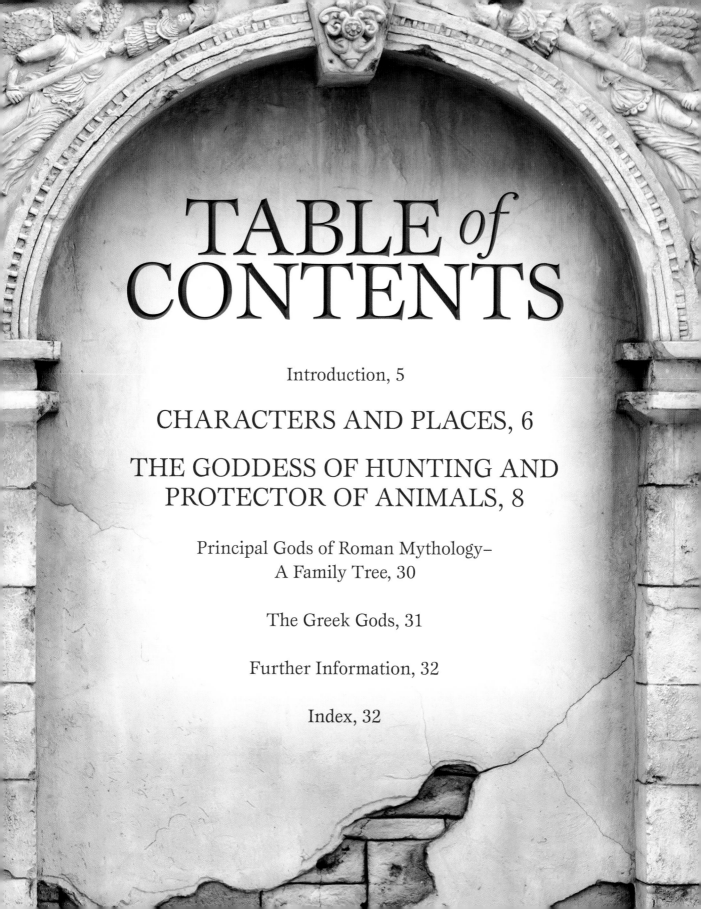

TABLE *of* CONTENTS

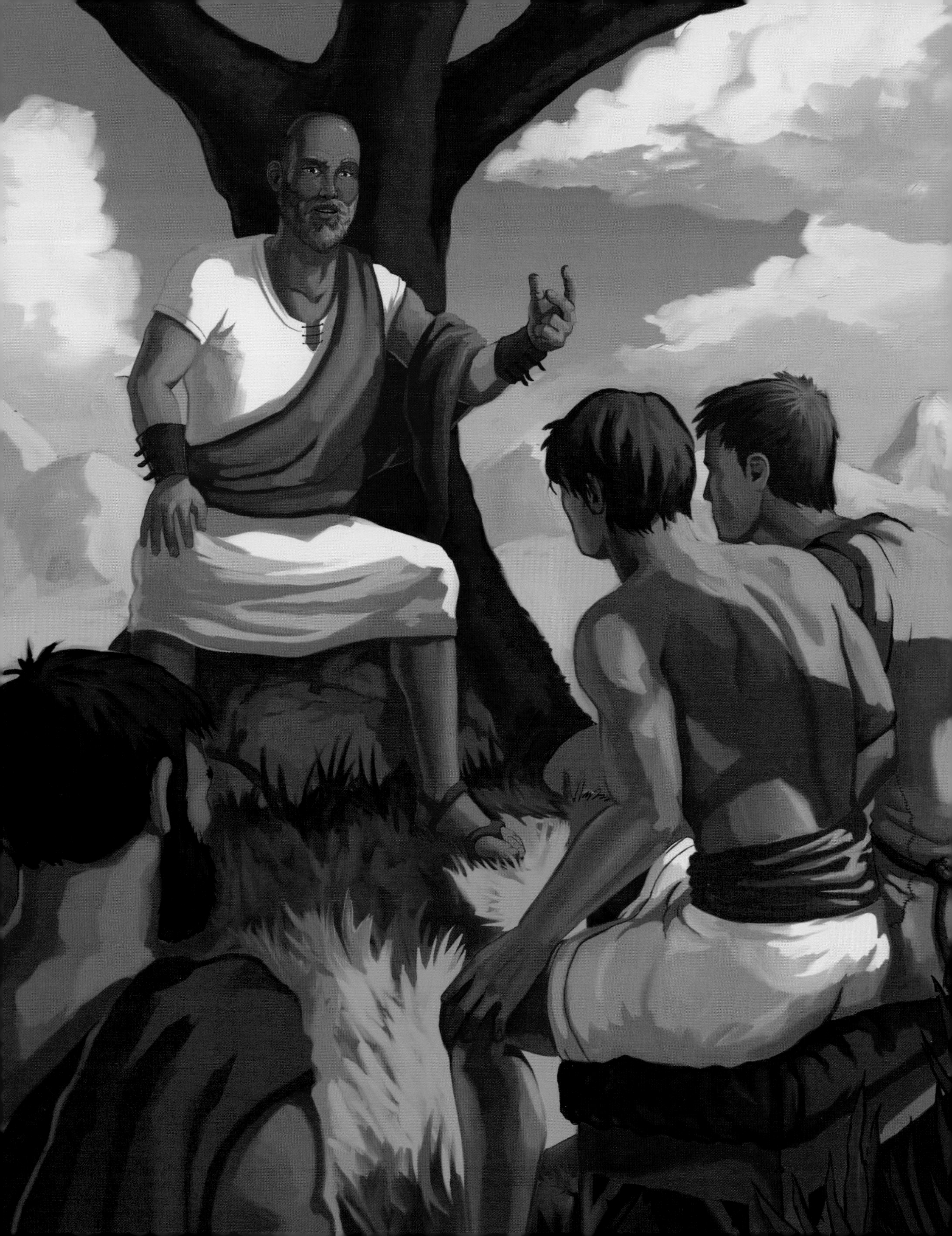

INTRODUCTION

In ancient times Romans believed in spirits or gods called numina. In Latin, *numina* means divine will or power. The Romans took part in religious rituals to please the gods. They felt the gods had powers that could make their lives better.

As the Roman government grew more powerful, its armies conquered many neighboring lands. Romans often adopted beliefs from these new cultures. They greatly admired the Greek arts and sciences. Gradually, the Romans combined the Greek myths and religion with their own. These stories shaped and influenced each part of a Roman citizen's daily life. Ancient Roman poets, such as Ovid and Virgil, wrote down these tales of wonder. Their writings became a part of Rome's great history. To the Romans, however, these stories were not just for entertainment. Roman mythology was their key to understanding the world.

ANCIENT ROMAN SOCIETIES

Ancient Roman society was divided into several groups. The patricians were the most powerful and wealthiest group. They often owned land and held power in the government. The plebeians worked for the patricians. Slaves were prisoners of war or children without parents. Some slaves were freed and enjoyed most of the rights of citizens.

CHARACTERS AND PLACES

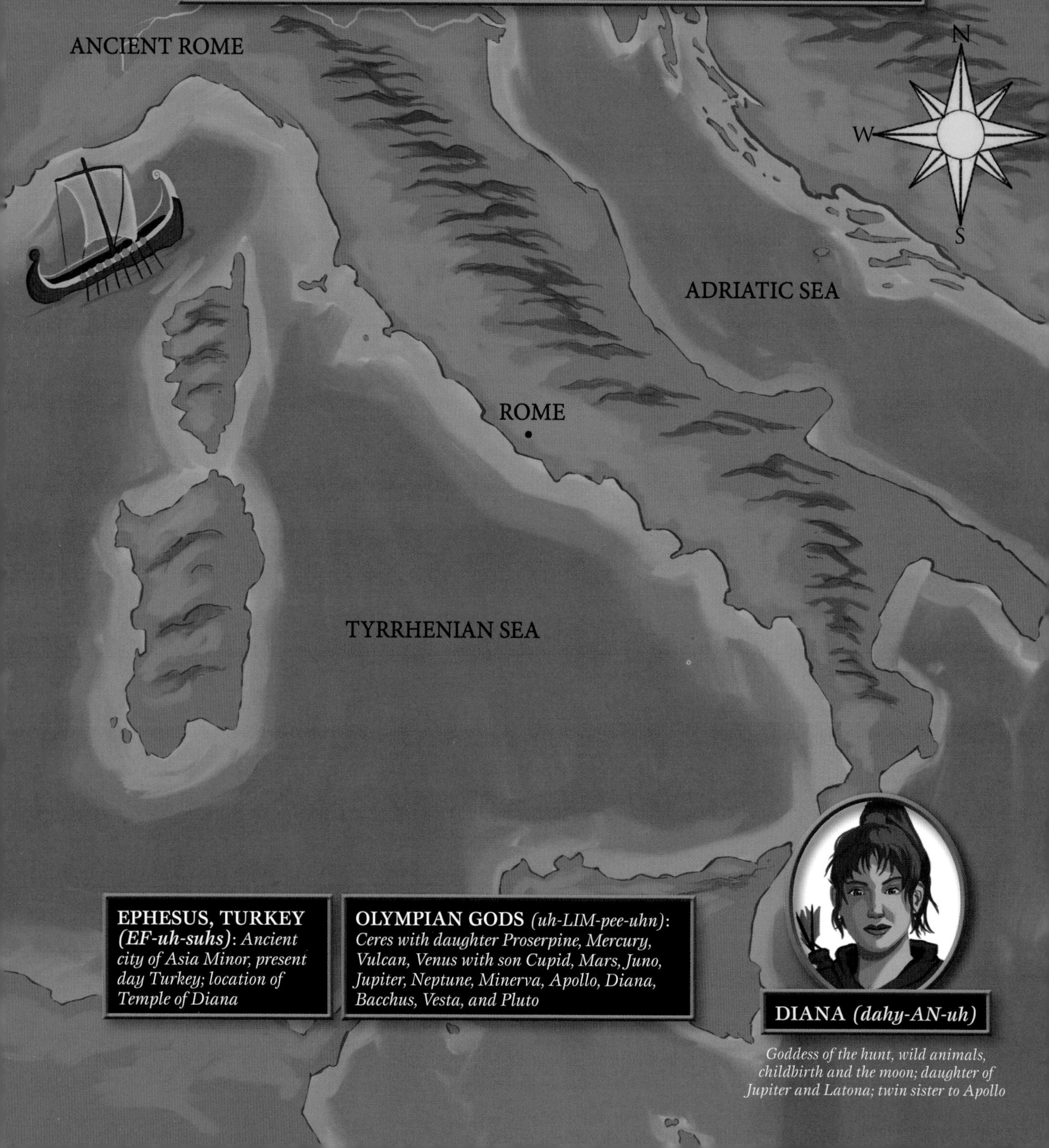
ANCIENT ROME
N
W
S
ADRIATIC SEA
ROME
TYRRHENIAN SEA

EPHESUS, TURKEY *(EF-uh-suhs)*: *Ancient city of Asia Minor, present day Turkey; location of Temple of Diana*

OLYMPIAN GODS *(uh-LIM-pee-uhn)*: *Ceres with daughter Proserpine, Mercury, Vulcan, Venus with son Cupid, Mars, Juno, Jupiter, Neptune, Minerva, Apollo, Diana, Bacchus, Vesta, and Pluto*

DIANA *(dahy-AN-uh)*

Goddess of the hunt, wild animals, childbirth and the moon; daughter of Jupiter and Latona; twin sister to Apollo

ACTAEON *(AK-tee-uhn)*

Hunter who Diana transformed into a stag

AGAMEMNON *(ag-uh-MEM-nahn)*

Leader of the Greek forces in the Trojan War

APOLLO *(a-POL-lo)*

God of sun, music, healing, and prophecy; son of Jupiter and Latona; twin to Diana

ARETHUSA *(ar-uh-THOO-zuh)*

A nymph who was changed into a spring to save her when she was being pursued by the river god Alpheus

ATALANTA *(at-l-AN-tuh)*

A Greek heroine who agreed to only marry the man who could beat her in a footrace

CALLISTO *(kuh-LIS-toh)*

A nymph attendant who Diana punished for a love affair with Jupiter

IPHIGENIA *(if-i-juh-NEE-uh)*

Daughter of King Agamemnon; sacrificed to appease the goddess Diana

JUNO *(JOO-noh)*

Queen of the gods; married to Jupiter

LATONA *(luh-TOH-nuh)*

Titan goddess; mother of Apollo and Diana

NIOBE *(NAHY-oh-bee)*

Queen of Thebes whose children were killed by Apollo and Diana as revenge for disrespecting their mother

OENEUS *(EE-nee-uhs)*

King who Diana punished for neglecting his worship

OTUS AND EPHIALTES *(OH-tuhs and eff-ee-ALL-tees)*

Enormous twin giants; sons of Neptune

THE GODDESS OF HUNTING AND PROTECTOR OF ANIMALS

The goddess Diana ruled over hunting, childbirth, and the moon. She was known for her strength and athleticism. Diana was an incredibly skilled hunter. She was also known for her beauty and grace. However, Diana's story was nearly stopped before it started.

High on a mountaintop, hidden behind snow and clouds, was a magnificent palace that was home to the Olympic gods and goddesses. This was Mount Olympus. The Olympic gods and goddesses ruled over the heavens and protected the earth. Their ruler was Jupiter. He was married to Juno. Everything at Mount Olympus should have been perfect. But it was far from that.

Jupiter wanted more wives so he could have many children. But Juno didn't want to share Jupiter. Afraid of Juno's anger, Jupiter snuck behind Juno's back to see other women. One goddess was Latona. Juno found out Jupiter and Latona had married and were pregnant with twins.

Juno became upset. She created a plan to get revenge. First Juno ordered all of the lands in the world to refuse Latona shelter. Then Juno sent her serpent to torment Latona. Chased from place to place, Latona thought she would never find a safe place to give birth to her twins.

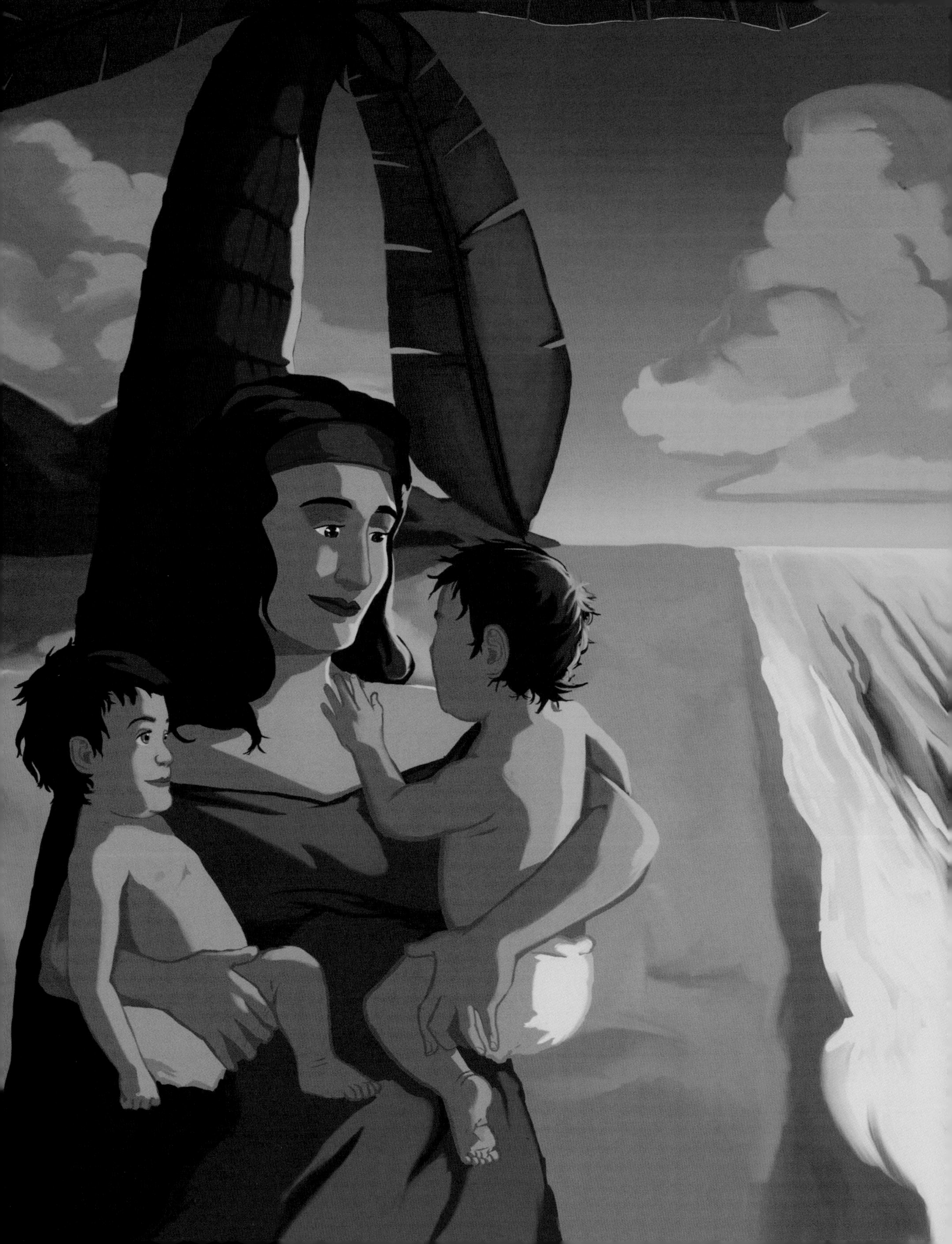

Neptune, the god of the seas, had made a new island for himself. It was called Delos. When Latona asked for shelter on Delos, she was welcomed. Latona relaxed in the shade of the island's palm tree. But the birth of the twins would not be easy for her.

Diana was born first. She had dark hair and was as lovely as the moon. After Diana was born, Latona was weary. She thought she could not continue. Diana helped Latona deliver the second baby.

It took nine days of labor before Apollo was born. He was beautiful. He became the god of the sun, music, healing, and prophecy.

Latona left the twins in the care of Themis, her aunt. Themis watched over the twins and nourished them with ambrosia and nectar. This was the food and drink of the gods. Jupiter was overjoyed by the twins' birth. They became two of his favorite children.

Jupiter loved his daughter Diana very much. He liked to spoil and shower her with gifts. Diana told him she never wanted to marry. She wanted to be a maiden forever. Diana requested 60 ocean nymphs to sing with her and 20 woodland nymphs to hunt with her. She wanted her special place to be the mountains.

Diana asked the Cyclopes to create a special silver bow and arrows for her. The Cyclopes were giant creatures with one eye in the middle of their foreheads.

NYMPHS AND FAUNS
Ancient Romans believed in many types of creatures. Nymphs were goddesses who watched over nature. They were beautiful and graceful maidens and were highly respected. Nymphs had very long lives, often serving as attendants to Olympic goddesses. Fauns were also woodland creatures. They were half man and half goat. Their father was Faunus, an ancient Latin king and a grandson of Saturn, who was king of the gods before Jupiter. Faunus was worshipped as a god of the forests and fields.

Cyclopes were skilled builders and craftsmen. The arrows were designed to give the animals she hunted a painless death. The Cyclopes also made Diana a magnificent golden chariot. Giant deer with golden antlers pulled the chariot through the woods and mountains.

Diana's other companions were beloved hunting dogs. The woodland god, Faunus, gave the dogs to Diana. They were faster than the wind and as fierce as lions.

Diana was also talented musically, like her brother Apollo. She loved to spend her time singing and dancing. Alongside her nymphs, Diana roamed the mountains and forests.

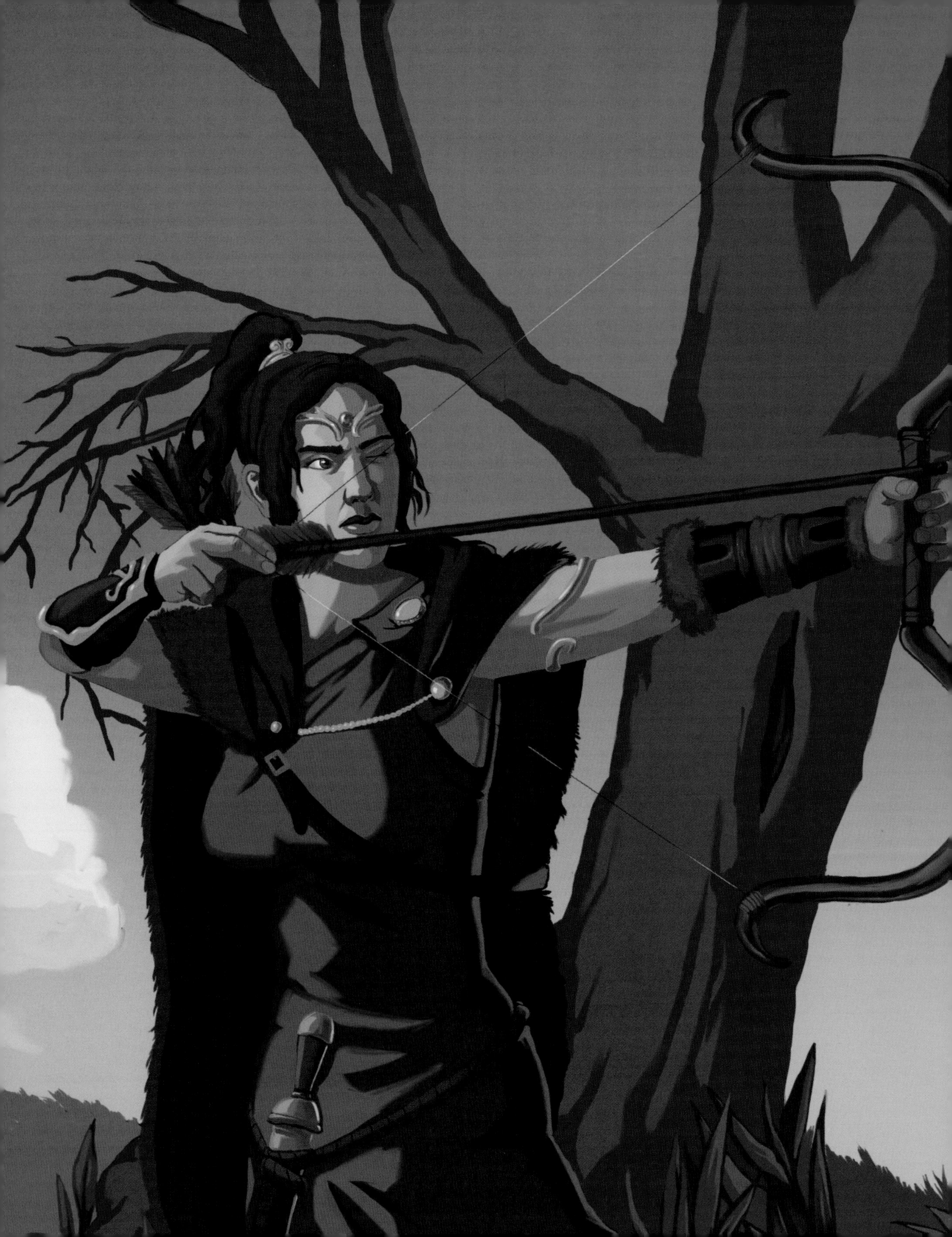

Diana was a tall and athletic dark-haired beauty. She was a popular subject in Roman art. She usually appeared as a huntress. Diana was often pictured wearing a hunting tunic and a crown on her brow. She held her bow and quiver of arrows in her hand. Diana was also usually seen with a hound or a deer.

As a goddess of fertility, Diana presided over childbirth, childrearing, and female development. Ancient Romans thought of her as a protector of children and the weak. Women prayed to Diana when they wanted to get pregnant and have an easy birth.

Diana was usually identified with the Greek goddess Artemis. Like her Greek counterpart, Diana was the goddess of domestic animals. She was offended if mortals neglected their livestock.

SELENE – GODDESS OF THE MOON

In Greek, the name Selene means "moon." Selene represented the moon in both Greek and Roman religion. At the new and full moons, Romans worshipped Selene. Her sister was Eos, the dawn. Her brother, Helios, was the sun god. By 400 BCE, Selene was identified with Artemis and Diana. She was often depicted as a woman driving a two-horse chariot with a moon in the background. The moon formed a crescent on her brow.

Diana lived a life without physical love, and she
required her attendants to do the same. She could be
very cruel to those who offended her. A nymph named
Callisto learned this the hard way. Jupiter fell in love

with Callisto. When Callisto became pregnant, Diana was furious. She turned Callisto into a bear.

Arethusa, another of Diana's followers, was hunting. Hot and tired, she decided to cool off in the Alpheus River in Greece. Alpheus was the god of that river. He took human form and began to chase Arethusa. Arethusa called to Diana. Diana turned Arethusa into a spring of water to save her. When Alpheus found Arethusa, Alpheus returned to water form. But Arethusa had disappeared under the earth. Diana had created a tunnel under the sea from Greece to Italy. The place in Italy where Arethusa's spring bubbles up became holy ground to Diana. Ancient legend claims if a wooden cup is thrown in the Alpheus River, it will later appear in Arethusa's well.

ECHO AND NARCISSUS
The nymph Echo was involved in another sad tale. She fell in love with a beautiful young man named Narcissus, but he rejected her. Diana punished him for his cruelty by making him fall in love with his own reflection. He spent each day staring at the pond. Echo kept Narcissus company. Legend says that Echo faded away until all that remained was her voice. Narcissus also wasted away and eventually died. All that was left behind was a white flower that now bears his name.

Diana was an independent goddess. She preferred to spend her time roaming the mountains and forests with her companion nymphs. Any unsuspecting intruders who did harm to her favorite animals were met with punishment.

Actaeon was one unlucky intruder. He was known for his great hunting skills. He spent his days wandering the forest with his dogs and companions. One day Actaeon came upon Diana as she was bathing. Diana was furious that a human had seen her naked body. In retaliation she immediately turned Actaeon into a stag. He was chased down and torn to pieces by his own dogs. Though she was beautiful, Diana's punishments were fierce.

King Oeneus learned that lesson as well when he made the mistake of neglecting Diana. Oeneus was so busy ruling his kingdom that one season he forgot to dedicate the first fruits of the harvest to Diana. Diana punished him by sending a monstrous boar to attack his lands and terrify his people. It became known as the Calydonian Boar.

From all over Greece, heroes came to hunt the boar. Atalanta, the only woman to arrive, was the first to

wound the animal. She had been abandoned at birth,
raised by a female bear, and protected by Diana as a
fellow child of the wood. When the boar was finally
killed, Atalanta was awarded its hide.

Diana and her twin brother Apollo were close siblings and friends. They were both skilled archers and liked to hunt together. The siblings were also fiercely loyal to their mother, Latona. Diana had the ability to bring prosperity and a long life to the humans she favored. However,

Diana was also vengeful. She could punish with plague and misfortune those who displeased her.

The queen of Thebes, Niobe, was another person to feel Diana's wrath. Niobe had six sons and six daughters. She boasted about the number of children she had during a ceremony meant to honor Latona. Niobe mocked the goddess for only having two children.

When Latona heard of Niobe's disrespect, she sent Apollo and Diana to take revenge. Apollo killed her six sons as they were practicing athletics. Diana then used her deadly bow and arrows to kill the daughters as they grieved over the deaths of their brothers. In shock, Niobe turned to stone. Endless tears flowed from the rock. To ancient people, Niobe was an eternal symbol of grief and sorrow.

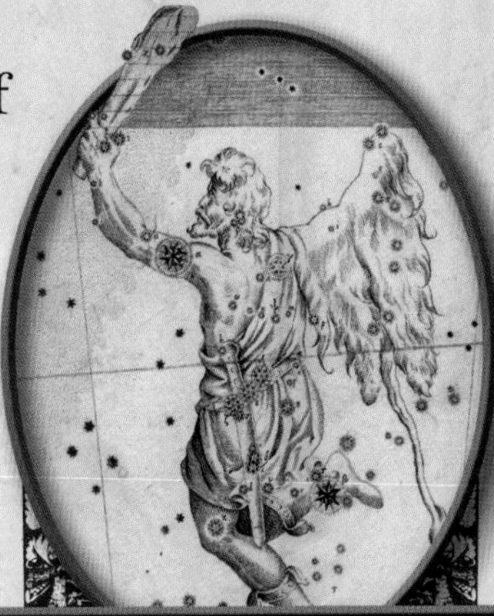

ORION

The giant Orion was another of Diana's hunting companions. He was handsome, lively, and a talented hunter. There are many legends about him, but all end in his untimely death. Diana is responsible for killing him. Some say Orion met his death after he bragged that he was going to kill all of the wild animals on the earth. Diana sent a scorpion after him that stung him to death. Diana had not meant to kill her friend. His death saddened her. She placed him in the sky as a constellation.

Diana also had trouble with Otus and Ephialtes.
They were twin sons of the sea god, Neptune. Otus and
Ephialtes decided it was time to look for wives. They

planned to kidnap the goddesses Juno and Diana and marry them, by force if necessary.

Otus chose Juno, since she was the queen of all gods. Ephialtes preferred Diana for her purity. They drew lots to see which should seize his lady first. Ephialtes won. They searched for Diana everywhere. They looked over the hills and deep in the woods but could not find her anywhere.

Eventually Otus and Ephialtes saw Diana running directly for the sea. All of Neptune's sons could run as easily on water as on land. So they chased Diana out into the sea. She led them to an island called Naxos. Then she disappeared.

Diana had turned herself into a white deer while the hunters looked away. She darted between the brothers and leapt into the forest. Otus and Ephialtes thought the deer was so beautiful, they completely forgot about searching for Diana. They lost sight of the deer and separated to find it. Both brothers found the deer. But they did not see each other before hurling their spears. Diana was quick. Their throws missed her, and the two giants hit each other instead. They both died.

In later myths, Diana became associated with the Greek goddess Hecate. Hecate was the goddess who presided over magic and spells. She was also goddess of the dark of the moon, when the moon was hidden. Hecate became associated with the deeds of darkness. She was also related to the crossroads, ghostly places where evil magic was practiced.

Diana was viewed as the goddess with three forms. *Triformis* was the Latin word Romans used to describe this. It means "threefold." The three parts were Selene as the sky, Diana as the earth, and Hecate as the lower world. Ancient people thought Diana's three sides showed that good and evil could be found in each of the gods.

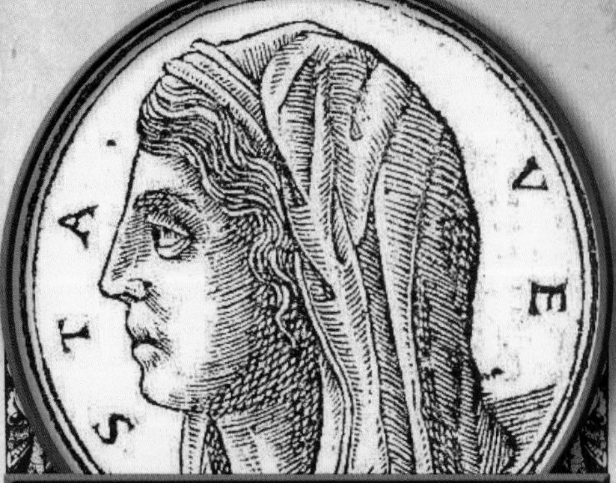
VESTA

VESTA – GODDESS OF THE HEARTH

In Roman religion, Vesta was the goddess of the hearth and home. Ancient people placed a lot of importance on keeping the hearth fire burning at all times. As a result, Vesta's worship was observed in every household. The Vestal Virgins, a group of priestesses, kept the sacred fire burning in Vesta's public temple. The bright fire thanked Vesta for her care of the people. If the fire ever went out accidentally, it was considered a warning of disaster to the city of Rome.

Often Diana was grouped with the goddesses Minerva and Vesta. All three were maidens who had sworn never to marry.

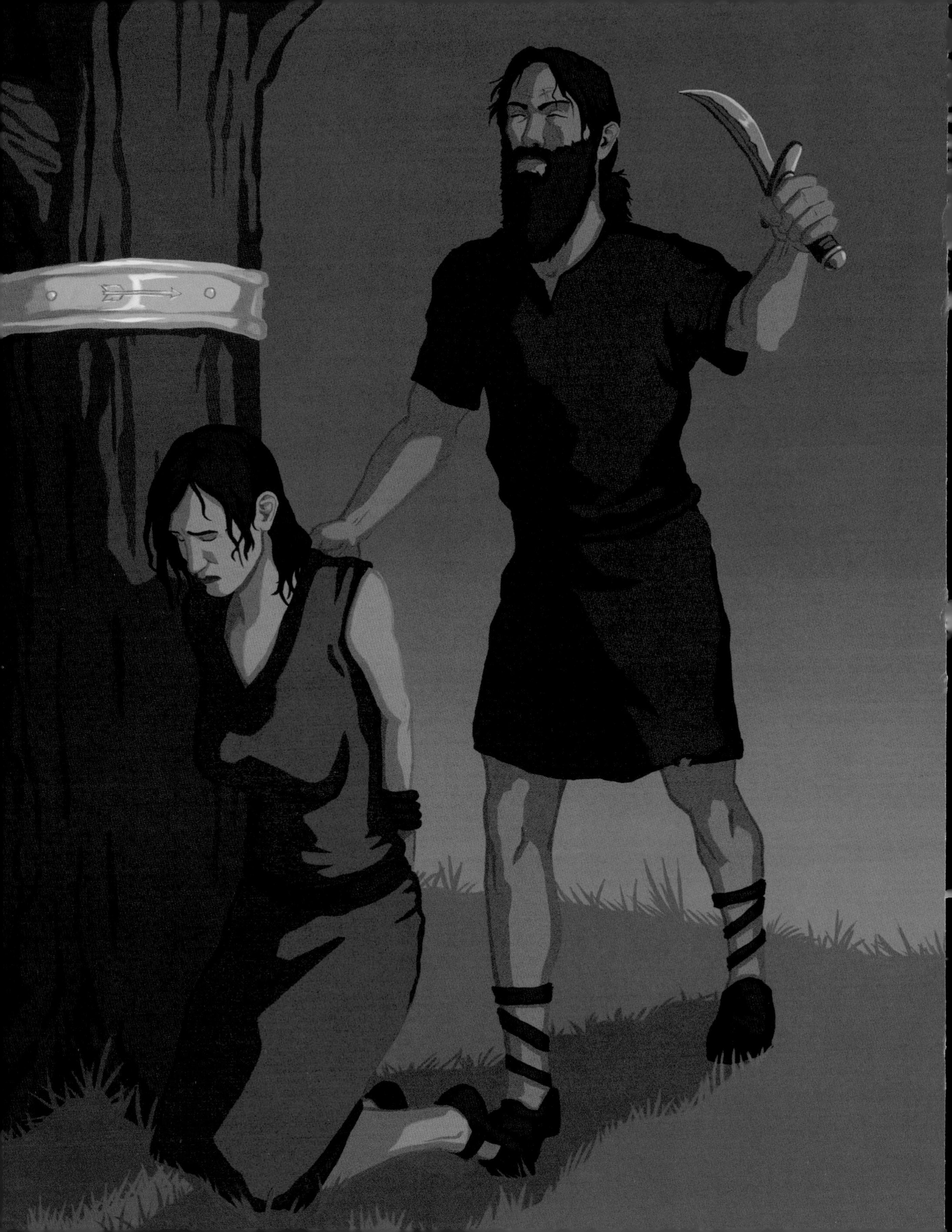

Another of Diana's penalties was given to King Agamemnon of Mycenae. The king was foolish. After killing a sacred deer, he boasted that he was a better hunter than Diana. Diana stranded his fleet of ships on the eve of the Trojan War.

A seer, one who predicts the future, told Agamemnon of his fate. He would need to sacrifice his daughter Iphigenia to Diana. This would please Diana. So Agamemnon tricked his daughter. He told her she was going to marry the hero Achilles.

According to ancient Roman tradition, Diana was a gentle and holy goddess who would never ask for the life of an innocent maiden. In the moment just before Iphigenia's death, Diana replaced Iphigenia with a deer. She then whisked Iphigenia off to become a priestess in Diana's temple. In some versions, Agamemnon killed his daughter when she arrived instead.

Diana was originally an Italian woodland goddess of fertility and nature. As her stories changed, she became the Roman goddess of hunting. Diana's most famous place of worship was an oak grove on the shores of Lake Nemi near Rome. Ancient Romans worshipped Diana and her servants, Egeria and Virbius. Egeria assisted Diana as a midwife. Virbius was a woodland god who was thought to be the first priest of Diana's temple.

TEMPLE AT EPHESUS
The Temple of Artemis was another important place where Diana was worshiped. It was built around 550 BCE in Ephesus, Turkey. The temple was famous for its beautiful artwork and its enormous size. It was considered one of the Seven Wonders of the Ancient World. A fire in 262 CE completely destroyed the temple. Only replicas of the statue that stood there have survived.

Diana's festival fell on August 13. This was the day King Servius Tullius, who was born a slave, dedicated Diana's temple in Rome. It was a day to worship Diana and a holiday for slaves. Diana had many good qualities. She was highly revered by ancient people, and she lives on in their myths and legends.

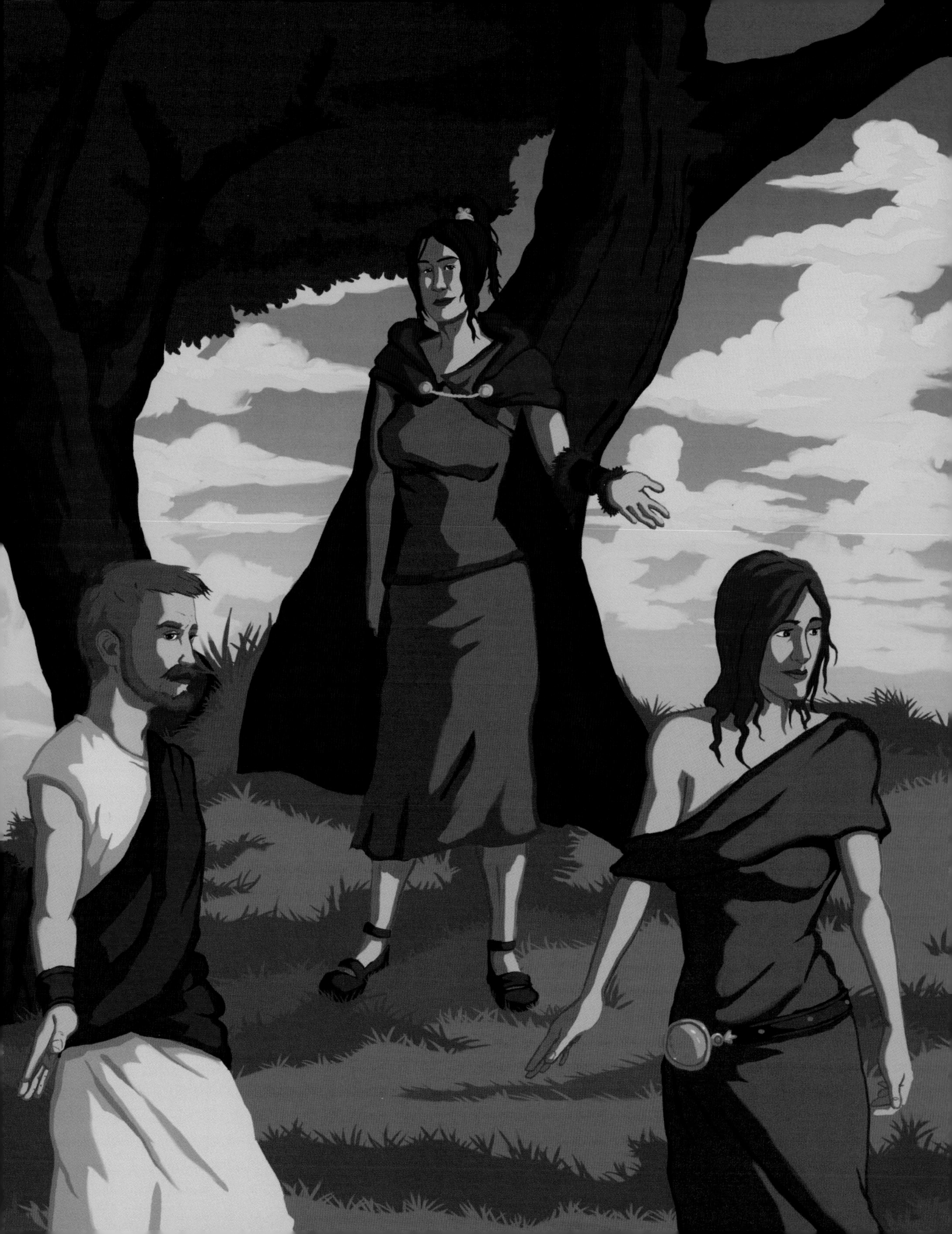

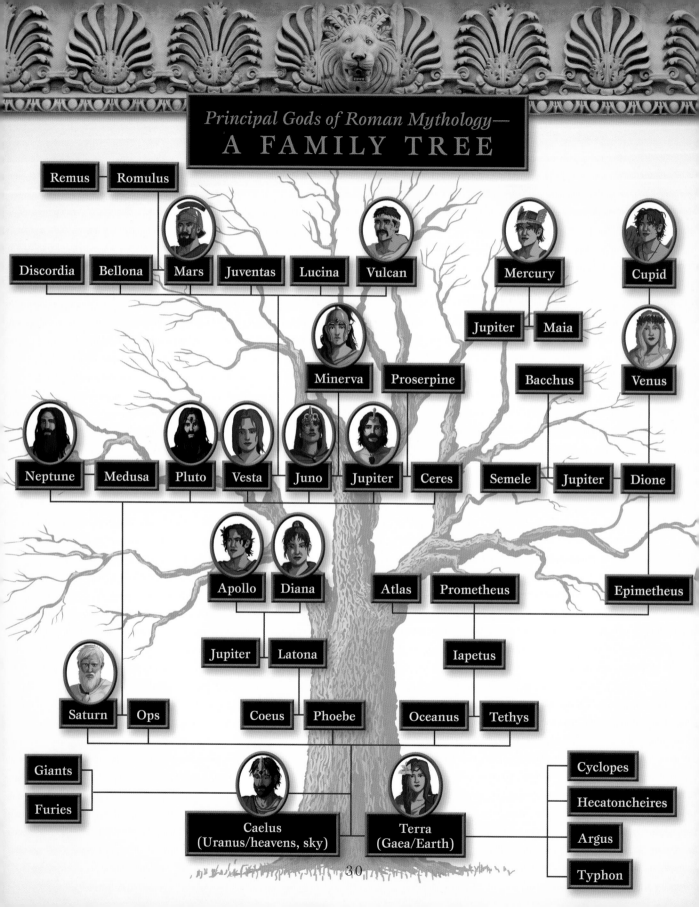

Principal Gods of Roman Mythology—
A FAMILY TREE

Remus — Romulus

Discordia — Bellona — Mars — Juventas — Lucina — Vulcan

Mercury

Cupid

Minerva — Proserpine

Jupiter — Maia

Bacchus

Venus

Neptune — Medusa — Pluto — Vesta — Juno — Jupiter — Ceres — Semele — Jupiter — Dione

Apollo — Diana

Atlas — Prometheus

Epimetheus

Jupiter — Latona

Iapetus

Saturn — Ops

Coeus — Phoebe

Oceanus — Tethys

Giants

Furies

Caelus
(Uranus/heavens, sky)

Terra
(Gaea/Earth)

Cyclopes

Hecatoncheires

Argus

Typhon

THE GREEK GODS

Ancient Greeks believed gods and goddesses ruled the world. The gods fell in love and struggled for power, but they never died. The ancient Greeks believed their gods were immortal. The Greek people worshiped the gods in temples. They felt the gods would protect and guide them. Over time, the Romans and many other cultures adopted the Greek myths as their own. While these other cultures changed the names of the gods, many of the stories remain the same.

SATURN: *Cronus*
God of Time and God of Sowing
Symbol: Sickle or Scythe

JUPITER: *Zeus*
King of the Gods, God of Sky, Rain, and Thunder
Symbols: Thunderbolt, Eagle, and Oak Tree

JUNO: *Hera*
Queen of the Gods, Goddess of Marriage,
*   Pregnancy, and Childbirth*
Symbols: Peacock, Cow, and Diadem
*   (Diamond Crown)*

NEPTUNE: *Poseidon*
God of the Sea
Symbols: Trident, Horse, and Dolphin

PLUTO: *Hades*
God of the Underworld
Symbols: Invisibility Helmet and Pomegranate

MINERVA: *Athena*
Goddess of Wisdom, War, and Arts and Crafts
Symbols: Owl, Shield, Loom, and Olive Tree

MARS: *Ares*
God of War
Symbols: Wild Boar, Vulture, and Dog

DIANA: *Artemis*
Goddess of the Moon and Hunt
Symbols: Deer, Moon, and Silver Bow and Arrows

APOLLO: *Apollo*
God of the Sun, Music, Healing, and Prophecy
Symbols: Laurel Tree, Lyre, Bow, and Raven

VENUS: *Aphrodite*
Goddess of Love and Beauty
Symbols: Dove, Swan, and Rose

CUPID: *Eros*
God of Love
Symbols: Bow and Arrows

MERCURY: *Hermes*
Messenger to the Gods, God of Travelers and Trade
Symbols: Crane, Caduceus, Winged Sandals,
*   and Helmet*

FURTHER INFORMATION

BOOKS

Johnson, Robin. *Understanding Roman Myths*. New York: Crabtree Publishing, 2012.

Temple, Teri. *Artemis: Goddess of Hunting and Protector of Animals*. Mankato, MN: Child's World, 2013.

WEB SITES

Visit our Web site for links about Diana: *childsworld.com/links*

Note to Parents, Teachers, and Librarians: We routinely verify our Web links to make sure they are safe and active sites. So encourage your readers to check them out!

INDEX